Rohan Goes to Big School

Pamela Mordecai
Illustrated by Avril Turner

Rohan sat all alone in the yard of Solina Infant School.

"I'm not going to big school tomorrow," he said to himself. "It's my birthday. I won't have a happy birthday if I go."

You had to be six years old to go to primary school so everyone called it "big school".

Rohan's new school was beautiful but he hated it.
Everything was too BIG.
The children and the teachers were big.
The school hall was huge.
And the cows next door were gigantic.

The breeze made Rohan drowsy.
Soon he was fast asleep.
Suddenly a voice boomed, "Here's a fine surprise!"
Rohan jumped up.
He saw Watchie, the watchman.
"Well, Rohan," said Watchie. "What brings you here?"
"I came to say goodbye," Rohan said. "I'm running away."

"Where are you headed?" Watchie asked.

"I'm taking the bus to town," said Rohan. "I'll hide on a ship and sail to Canada."

"Do you have everything you need?" asked Watchie.

"I've got some food," said Rohan. "And clothes and a little money."

"You'll need lots of food," said Watchie. "And a warm coat. It's cold in Canada."

"I'll go with you to the bus," said Watchie. Rohan was worried.

"Where will I get money for a coat?" he wondered.

At the bus stop, Watchie said, "Goodbye, Rohan. Send me a postcard."

As soon as Watchie walked off, Rohan ran straight home.

The next day Rohan's Mom woke him early.
"Happy birthday, son," she said.
"Thanks, Mom," said Rohan.
    Then he asked, "Do I have to go to school?"
"Don't worry," said his Mom. "You will make
    lots of new friends."
"Suppose I don't?" asked Rohan.
"You will," said his Mom. "Now, hurry.
    Breakfast is ready."

Rohan hurried into the kitchen.

"Happy birthday, son," said his Dad.

"Close your eyes and hold out your hands," said his Mom.

Rohan felt something heavy.

"Now open them," said his Dad.

Rohan was holding a beautiful cricket bat.

"Thanks, Mom. Thanks, Dad," he said.

"Take it to school," his Dad said. "Play cricket with your friends."

Rohan's Dad stopped his truck at the school gate.
Inside Rohan could see hundreds of boys and
girls.
Some were talking and laughing.
Some just stood quietly looking around.
Rohan climbed out of the truck slowly.

"Don't forget your bat," said his Dad.

"We'll come in with you, if you want," said his Mom.

"No thanks," said Rohan. "Goodbye, Mom and Dad."

And he walked into big school by himself.

Rohan didn't see one friendly face.
Then three big boys came towards him.
"Isn't this a nice bat, Hulk?" said the tallest one.
"It's beautiful, Longers," Hulk replied.
"Shall we borrow it, Strongboy?" Longers asked
the third boy.
"Yeah," said Strongboy, laughing wickedly. "We
could borrow it for keeps!"

Rohan was scared. There was no one to help him.
At that minute the school bell rang.
Teachers came from nowhere.
They hurried the children into the hall.
"Come on, fellows," Hulk said, "we'll get the bat later."
The three boys walked away and Rohan flew into the hall.

At lunch time, Rohan stayed inside.
He didn't want to lose his bat.
After a while, the boy who sat beside Rohan
came back in.
His name was Carl.
Carl opened his desk and took out a ball.
"Look, Rohan," he said, "we can play cricket."

"There's Ava," said Carl waving at a little
girl with lots of plaits.

"Hi, Carl," said Ava.

"This is Rohan," said Carl. "He has a new bat."

"It's beautiful," Ava said. "Can we play with it?"

"I guess so," said Rohan, looking around
anxiously.

"You bat, Carl," said Rohan. "I'll bowl."

"I'll get the ball," said Ava.

Rohan bowled.

Carl hit the ball hard and started to run.

He didn't get far.

Ava ran as fast as a mongoose.

She swooped down, grabbed the ball, and turned to throw it.

Carl scooted back to the wicket.

Just then, Longers, Strongboy, and Hulk walked over.

"Give me the bat," Hulk said.

"It's not mine," Carl said. "You have to ask Rohan."

Rohan saw how big the three boys were. He was small. So were his friends.

"You can have a turn," said Rohan.

Rohan bowled his best ball to Hulk.
He hoped it would smash into the wicket and
bowl Hulk out.
Instead Hulk hit the ball with all his might into
the cow pen.
It soared into the air and landed right in front
of the bull.

"What a shot!" said Hulk, "I'm the greatest batsman ever."

"Aren't you going to get the ball?" asked Ava. "You hit it into the cow pen."

"It's your job to catch the ball," Hulk replied.

"It's all right, Ava," Carl said. "I'll go."

"Me too," said Rohan.

The boys climbed into the cow pen.
"Cows are gentle," Carl said. "They only
attack if you scare them."
"I'm too small to scare a cow," Rohan said.
"I'll go up to him," Carl said. "When he's
looking at me, grab the ball."
Carl walked towards the bull while Rohan
crept up and got the ball.

As they walked back, Hulk yelled, "I'm ready for the second ball."

Ava ran up to Carl and Rohan.

"I want to bowl," she said.

"Can you bowl?" asked Rohan.

"You'll see," said Ava.

Rohan gave Ava the ball and she walked to the end of the pitch.

Suddenly they saw a little red rocket racing towards Hulk.

Hulk waved his bat, but the ball whizzed past him, hitting the wicket and knocking a stump flat.

"Bowled!" Ava shouted.

"Great ball!" shouted Rohan and Carl.

Strongboy grabbed the bat from Hulk.
"You can't bowl me out," he yelled at Ava.
Ava ran slowly this time.
She threw the ball, and it curled gently
through the air.
Strongboy hit it.
It curled back, right into Ava's hands.
"Out!" shouted Rohan and Carl.

Ava took the bat from Strongboy and handed
it to Longers.

"Ready for your medicine?" she asked.

"Come on, fellows," said Longers. "We don't
have to play with a girl."

"You're just big bullies," said Ava. "I'm small
but I can bowl you out any time. I've been
playing cricket since the day I was born!"

After school, Carl and Ava walked home with Rohan, and his Mom let them in.

"Surprise!" shouted all Rohan's friends from Solina Infant School.

There was a birthday cake and ice cream and curried chicken.

Everyone sang 'Happy Birthday'.

Then Rohan and Carl said, "A big cheer for Ava, the best bowler in Solina!"

Hip, hip, hooray! everyone shouted.

"Thanks, everybody," Ava said. "Now, why don't we play cricket?"